Poetry for Young People

Wallace Stevens

Edited by John N. Serio

Illustrations by Robert Gantt Steele

Sterling Publishing Co., Inc.
New York

For my children and for Sheila Barry, an editor's editor.

—John N. Serio

To my son Tyler. May you always see poetry in everyday things.

—Robert Gantt Steele

Library of Congress Cataloging-in-Publication Data

Stevens, Wallace, 1879–1955.
  [Poems. Selections]
  Wallace Stevens / edited by John N. Serio ; illustrations by Robert Gantt Steele.
      p. cm. -- (Poetry for young people)
  Includes index.
  ISBN 1-4027-0925-0
  1. Children's poetry, American. I. Serio, John N., 1943– II. Steele, Robert
Gantt. III. Title. IV. Series.
  PS3537.T4753A6 2004
  811'.52—dc22   2004013444

The photograph of Wallace Stevens on page 4 is from the Wallace Stevens Papers
(Box 67[1]), Huntington Library, San Marino, Calif. Reproduced by permission.
"A Rabbit as King of the Ghosts" and "The House Was Quiet and the World Was
Calm" from *The Collected Poems of Wallace Stevens* by Wallace Stevens, copyright
1954 by Wallace Stevens and renewed 1982 by Holly Stevens. Used by permission
of Alfred A. Knopf, a division of Random House, Inc. Quotations from Wallace
Stevens in the editorial material come from *Letters of Wallace Stevens,* edited by
Holly Stevens (New York: Alfred A. Knopf, 1966); *Opus Posthumous,* edited by
Milton J. Bates (New York: Alfred A. Knopf, 1989); *Parts of a World: Wallace Stevens
Remembered, An Oral Biography* by Peter Brazeau (New York: Random House,
1983); and *Souvenirs and Prophecies: The Young Wallace Stevens* by Holly Stevens (New
York: Alfred A. Knopf, 1977).

2   4   6   8   10   9   7   5   3   1

Published by Sterling Publishing Co., Inc.
387 Park Avenue South, New York, NY 10016
Text © 2004 by John N. Serio
Illustrations © 2004 by Robert Gantt Steele
Distributed in Canada by Sterling Publishing
c/o Canadian Manda Group, One Atlantic Avenue, Suite 105
Toronto, Ontario, Canada M6K 3E7
Distributed in Great Britain and Europe by Chris Lloyd at Orca Book
Services, Stanley House, Fleets Lane, Poole BH15 3AJ, England
Distributed in Australia by Capricorn Link (Australia) Pty. Ltd.
P.O. Box 704, Windsor, NSW 2756, Australia

Manufactured in China
All rights reserved

Sterling ISBN 1-4027-0925-0

CONTENTS

INTRODUCTION

Imagine walking through a country field one peaceful, summer afternoon. The grass is high, the trees on the left sway in the breeze, the cloudless sky looks like a blue glass bowl. Without thinking of anything in particular, you take another step and BAM! an explosion of sound and color—you hear a thumping of wings, see a blur of glittering greens and blues, glistening yellows and reds, swirls of browns tipped with black. Your heart pounds with excitement and you feel a rush of joy as you watch a ring-necked pheasant fly out of sight. You can't wait to tell your parents and friends.

That's what Wallace Stevens meant when he said "A poem is a pheasant" and described poetry as "a pheasant disappearing in the brush." Stevens believed that poetry is an expression of feeling, a rare glimpse into one of life's secrets, a living moment filled with color and sound and texture and movement. Such an experience can recharge your life, giving it meaning and purpose. Usually, in Stevens, these are happy occurrences, but occasionally they can be sad. Stevens knew that life is not always cheerful and that it sometimes includes pain or loss. He believed poetry helps people to live their lives, for it comforts them during sorrow and releases joy during happiness.

Wallace Stevens was born on October 2, 1879, in Reading, Pennsylvania, the second son of Margaretha, a former teacher, and Garrett Stevens, a successful lawyer and businessman. As a child, Stevens played with his two brothers, Garrett, Jr., and John, who were all close in age. Like most boys, they could be mischievous. On one occasion, they were discovered stealing fruit from a neighbor's tree and ran away shouting, "God helps those who help themselves!" Stevens also had two younger sisters, Elizabeth and Mary Katharine.

Stevens' father was a hard worker and, as both a lawyer and a businessman, he provided well for his family (for a while, all three boys were in college at the same time). On Sundays, his mother played piano and sang hymns, and every evening she lulled the children to sleep by reading Bible stories. Stevens believed that he got his practical side from his father and his imaginative side from his mother.

As a young boy, Stevens got up early during summer vacation and took long walks before breakfast. He noticed the smallest details, such as "a huge cob-web between the rails of a fence sparkling with dew." He loved to swim—"I could swim for hours without resting," he recalled. When he rode his bicycle to a neighboring town, he felt a sense of adventure, as though he had just explored "unmapped country." He even had a "pirate period."

When Stevens discovered books, "many things changed," he said. He used to read late into the night, and he began to study hard—very hard. After going to private elementary schools, he attended Reading Boys' High School. "I took *all* the prizes at school!" he later told his fiancée. In his junior year, he won a prize for the best essay, and in his senior year received a gold medal for delivering a speech he had written about the self-made man and the importance of opportunity. His fellow students were proud of him, and when he received his medal, they gave him the school cheer. But Stevens wasn't all work and no play: he was also on the football team, played guitar, and sang in the choir.

Stevens attended Harvard College for three years to prepare for a professional career. But deep down he wanted to be a poet. As a student, he published poems and stories in Harvard's literary magazine and served as president of the literary society. In 1900 he moved to New York to try his hand at journalism, but he was neither happy nor successful. Although he wanted to take time off to become a poet, his father convinced him to attend law school. Like his father and two brothers, Stevens became a lawyer. Like them, he believed he needed to get a good job to support himself and a future family.

While working at various law firms in New York, Stevens couldn't wait for the weekends, for he still loved to take long walks. On Sunday mornings, he would get up early and follow the Hudson River into the countryside, walking twenty, thirty, and one time even more than forty miles in one day! These hikes not only invigorated him physically but also gave him time to "think over a thousand and one odds and ends," he wrote in his journal. He was keenly observant, and details of nature—the rare and delicate colors of wild flowers, various shades of green on fluttering leaves, changing cloud formations, the roar of a gushing stream, or the tranquility of a field—entered his poems.

On a visit home to Reading, in 1904, Stevens fell in love with Elsie Kachel, the prettiest girl in town, he recalled. They carried on their courtship through letters during the five years before they were married in 1909. Thoughts of Elsie inspired Stevens to write poetry. On two of her birthdays he presented her with booklets of poems he had composed. A number of years later, when he started to publish poetry in magazines, he used some of these poems and Elsie was hurt, for she felt they were personal. In 1914, Adolph Weinman, their landlord and a noted sculptor, asked Elsie to pose for a statue he wanted to enter in a design contest for American coins, and he won. If you want to see what Mrs. Stevens looked like, find a Mercury dime or a Walking Liberty half-dollar. They were minted between 1916 and the mid-1940s.

In 1916, Stevens accepted a position as a lawyer with the Hartford Accident and Indemnity Company, and he and Elsie moved from New York to Hartford, Connecticut, where they remained for the rest of their lives. Around this time, he started publishing poems in literary magazines, and in 1923 he gathered them together for his first book, *Harmonium*, named after a musical instrument. He was nearly forty-four years old. In 1924, his only child, a daughter named Holly, was born.

For the next six years, Stevens did not write much poetry. He focused his energies on his family and work, and in 1934 he became a vice president of the insurance company. Although he accomplished his goal of providing a comfortable living for his family, he remained a private and solitary person. He was not emotionally close to his relatives in Reading or even to his wife and daughter. Once, when his daughter asked why three people needed such a large house, he responded, "To be together when we wish" and then he added, "and to get away when we wish."

Around 1930, Stevens started publishing poems again in magazines and continued writing poetry for the rest of his life. New books appeared regularly: *Ideas of Order* (1935); *Owl's Clover* (1936); *The Man with the Blue Guitar and Other Poems* (1937); *Parts of a World* (1942); *Transport to Summer* (1947); and *The Auroras of Autumn* (1950). When *The Collected Poems of Wallace Stevens* was issued in 1954, it contained a section of twenty-five new poems. Stevens was seventy-five years old! He won many awards for his poetry, including the Bollingen Prize in Poetry, the National Book Award (twice), and the Pulitzer Prize. He also wrote essays on the art and importance of poetry and kept a journal. One of his entries tells us how to read a poem: "In poetry, you must love the words, the ideas and images and rhythms with all your capacity to love anything at all."

As a lawyer for the Hartford, Stevens traveled extensively throughout the United States. Many of the places he visited, such as Oklahoma, Tennessee, and Florida, provided settings for his poems (see "Life Is Motion," "Anecdote of the Jar," and "The Load of Sugar-Cane," pages 18, 19, and 22). Although he never traveled abroad, he had a great interest in learning about different cultures and enjoyed corresponding with people in other countries. He would ask people who lived or were traveling abroad to purchase items for him, and he was especially delighted when tea arrived from China, a statue of Buddha from Ceylon, or a painting from France. These items conveyed an essential part of their culture to Stevens, and they stimulated his imagination. They, too, found their way into his poems.

Stevens continued his favorite form of physical and mental exercise by walking two miles to work every day. While doing so, he would compose poetry in his head and then dictate the lines to his secretary. Working busily in his office, with dozens of open law books scattered about his desk and chairs, or dictating a letter, he would sometimes stop abruptly, open his lower right-hand desk drawer, and jot down a few lines on a piece of paper. Strolling with a friend during the lunch hour, he would pause and say, "Wait just a minute, please," and then take an envelope from his pocket and write down some lines. Even in the company of others, he seemed to live in a world of his own (see "Tea at the Palaz of Hoon," page 32, and "The House Was Quiet and the World Was Calm," page 46).

Although Stevens remained a businessman all his life—he never retired, even though he was nearly seventy-six years old when he died on August 2, 1955—he thought of himself primarily as a poet. Once, when someone asked him why he wrote poetry, he responded: "I feel very much like the boy whose mother told him to stop sneezing; he replied: 'I am not sneezing; it's sneezing me.'"

FROM A JUNK

What does the moon look like to you, when you see it shining over the ocean? It reminds the poet of a fish diving in the choppy water at night.

A great fish plunges in the dark,
Its fins of rutted silver; sides,
Belabored with a foamy light;
And back, brilliant with scaly salt.
It glistens in the flapping wind,
Burns there and glistens, wide and wide,
Under the five-horned stars of night,
In wind and wave . . . It is the moon.

Junk—*a type of Chinese sailboat*
rutted—*grooved*
belabored—*beaten upon soundly or excessively*

SONG

Wearing her Sunday best makes this little girl feel special.

There are great things doing
In the world,
Little rabbit.
There is a damsel,
Sweeter than the sound of the willow,
Dearer than shallow water
Flowing over pebbles.
Of a Sunday,
She wears a long coat,
With twelve buttons on it.
Tell that to your mother.

DISILLUSIONMENT OF TEN O'CLOCK

These grown-ups are boring. They go to bed every night at the same time. Even their dreams lack excitement, especially compared with the dreams of an old sailor. Are these people really alive? In their white nightgowns, they look like ghosts!

The houses are haunted
By white night-gowns.
None are green,
Or purple with green rings,
Or green with yellow rings,
Or yellow with blue rings.
None of them are strange,
With socks of lace
And beaded ceintures.
People are not going
To dream of baboons and periwinkles.
Only, here and there, an old sailor,
Drunk and asleep in his boots,
Catches tigers
In red weather.

Disillusionment—*free of a false belief*
ceintures—*belts or sashes worn around the waist*
periwinkles—*wild blue or white flowers, or snails*

EARTHY ANECDOTE

What is a firecat? You won't find the word in a dictionary. Stevens uses this made-up word to convey excitement and energy. Whenever the firecat jumps in the way of the disorderly herd, it forces the animals to form an orderly line. Could the firecat be the imagination?

Every time the bucks went clattering
Over Oklahoma
A firecat bristled in the way.

Wherever they went,
They went clattering,
Until they swerved
In a swift, circular line
To the right,
Because of the firecat.

Or until they swerved
In a swift, circular line
To the left,
Because of the firecat.

The bucks clattered.
The firecat went leaping,
To the right, to the left,
And
Bristled in the way.

Later, the firecat closed his bright eyes
And slept.

Anecdote—*a short story about an interesting or amusing incident*
bristled—*took an aggressive position, with hair standing on end*
bucks—*male deer or antelope*

THIRTEEN WAYS OF LOOKING AT A BLACKBIRD

Did you ever think you could look at a blackbird thirteen different ways? This poem suggests that if there are thirteen ways, there must be even more. In fact, there are countless ways to view not only a blackbird, but also everything in life. Each part of this poem presents the blackbird in a different setting, and that changes our response to it. Our imagination has to be nimble (like the firecat, page 12) to keep up with the sudden swings between far and near, large and tiny, before and after, etc. But with each new way of looking at the blackbird, we experience new sensations and new thoughts.

I

Among twenty snowy mountains,
The only moving thing
Was the eye of the blackbird.

II

I was of three minds,
Like a tree
In which there are three blackbirds.

III

The blackbird whirled in the autumn winds.
It was a small part of the pantomime.

IV

A man and a woman
Are one.
A man and a woman and a blackbird
Are one.

pantomime—*telling a story by bodily gestures only, as in a dance*

V

I do not know which to prefer,
The beauty of inflections
Or the beauty of innuendoes,
The blackbird whistling
Or just after.

VI

Icicles filled the long window
With barbaric glass.
The shadow of the blackbird
Crossed it, to and fro.
The mood
Traced in the shadow
An indecipherable cause.

VII

O thin men of Haddam,
Why do you imagine golden birds?
Do you not see how the blackbird
Walks around the feet
Of the women about you?

VIII

I know noble accents
And lucid, inescapable rhythms;
But I know, too,
That the blackbird is involved
In what I know.

inflections—*noticeable changes, usually in the sound of a word or its form*
innuendoes—*hints or suggestions*
barbaric—*uncivilized, unruly; here, primitive and distorted*
indecipherable—*cannot determine meaning*
Haddam—*a town in Connecticut*
lucid—*clear to understand*
inescapable—*cannot be avoided or denied*

IX

When the blackbird flew out of sight,
It marked the edge
Of one of many circles.

X

At the sight of blackbirds
Flying in a green light,
Even the bawds of euphony
Would cry out sharply.

XI

He rode over Connecticut
In a glass coach.
Once, a fear pierced him,
In that he mistook
The shadow of his equipage
For blackbirds.

XII

The river is moving.
The blackbird must be flying.

XIII

It was evening all afternoon.
It was snowing
And it was going to snow.
The blackbird sat
In the cedar-limbs.

bawds—*those who have sold out at lesser value, lowering their self-esteem or character*
euphony—*pleasing or sweet sound*
equipage—*horse-drawn carriage or coach*

THE INDIGO GLASS IN THE GRASS

When looked at closely, even ordinary objects become extraordinary.

Which is real—
This bottle of indigo glass in the grass,
Or the bench with the pot of geraniums, the stained mattress and the
    washed overalls drying in the sun?
Which of these truly contains the world?

Neither one, nor the two together.

indigo—*deep reddish blue*
geraniums—*flowers*

LIFE IS MOTION

Bonnie and Josie are so happy to be alive that they sing and dance around the stump of a dead tree. Even their song sounds something like their home state, Oklahoma. Count the number of words before and after the stump. What do you discover?

In Oklahoma,
Bonnie and Josie,
Dressed in calico,
Danced around a stump.
They cried,
"Ohoyaho,
Ohoo" . . .
Celebrating the marriage
Of flesh and air.

calico—*a heavy cloth made of cotton,*
   often containing a pattern

18

ANECDOTE OF THE JAR

Who wins this curious contest between a jar and a hill, between an object made by people and nature? In poetry it is important to look carefully at the words a poet chooses. At first, the jar seems successful because it tames the wilderness. But then it seems lifeless. The jar "makes" and "takes," but the wilderness "gives."

I placed a jar in Tennessee,
And round it was, upon a hill.
It made the slovenly wilderness
Surround that hill.

The wilderness rose up to it,
And sprawled around, no longer wild.
The jar was round upon the ground
And tall and of a port in air.

It took dominion everywhere.
The jar was gray and bare.
It did not give of bird or bush,
Like nothing else in Tennessee.

slovenly—*messy, lazy*
sprawled—*lying with arms and legs spread out*

THE PLOT AGAINST THE GIANT

Like David confronting Goliath, these three girls are going to defeat a giant, but they are going to do it with beauty—sweet-smelling flowers, tiny colors on cloths, and lovely words. This will make the crude giant sensitive to the beautiful world he has so carelessly tromped through.

First Girl
When this yokel comes maundering,
Whetting his hacker,
I shall run before him,
Diffusing the civilest odors
Out of geraniums and unsmelled flowers.
It will check him.

Second Girl
I shall run before him,
Arching cloths besprinkled with colors
As small as fish-eggs.
The threads
Will abash him.

Third Girl
Oh, la . . . le pauvre!
I shall run before him,
With a curious puffing.
He will bend his ear then.
I shall whisper
Heavenly labials in a world of gutturals.
It will undo him.

yokel—*a naive or gullible person from the country*
maundering—*wandering slowly and idly; grumbling*
hacker—*cutting tool*
diffusing—*spreading freely*
abash—*embarrass*
le pauvre—*French, "the poor thing"*
labials—*uttered with the lips; smooth-sounding words*
gutturals—*unpleasant, throaty sounds*

20

THE LOAD OF SUGAR-CANE

Imagine gliding through the Florida Everglades on a silent, pole-driven boat and noticing the resemblance between things: how the color of the water contains the color of the sky; how the green of the water grasses resembles the green of the surrounding trees. These similarities illustrate continuity in a constantly changing world. Noticing such resemblances, the poem suggests, can enrich our lives. We are surprised when the rainbows, which sweep across the sky like colorful birds, unexpectedly become real birds as they screech and fly at the boatman's red headdress.

The going of the glade-boat
Is like water flowing;

Like water flowing
Through the green saw-grass,
Under the rainbows;

Under the rainbows
That are like birds,
Turning, bedizened,

While the wind still whistles
As kildeer do,

When they rise
At the red turban
Of the boatman.

glade-boat—*a flat-bottomed boat used to navigate the Florida
  Everglades*

saw-grass—*tall grass that grows in a marsh and that has sharp, tiny
  teeth on its edges*

bedizened—*ornately dressed*

kildeer—*a robin-sized shoreline bird belonging to the plover family,
  characterized by two black breast bands and a penetrating cry; usually
  spelled killdeer*

TEA

Have you ever felt warm and cozy drinking a cup of hot chocolate indoors while a storm raged outdoors? As winter approaches, this person enjoys a cup of tea in a parlor and feels transported to a tropical paradise.

When the elephant's-ear in the park
Shrivelled in frost,
And the leaves on the paths
Ran like rats,
Your lamp-light fell
On shining pillows,
Of sea-shades and sky-shades,
Like umbrellas in Java.

elephant's-ear—*a plant with leaves that seem*
as large as elephants' ears
Java—*a tropical island in the South Pacific*

24

NUANCES OF A THEME BY WILLIAMS

This poem says, "Be yourself!" Stevens quotes in italics William Carlos Williams' poem "El Hombre" ("The Man") and then expands upon Williams' theme of courage. Both poets use the image of the morning star, which can still be seen next to the bright rising sun, to celebrate individuality. Stevens goes further than Williams by telling the star to remain brave and independent. The star should not allow anyone to change it by projecting his or her feelings onto it.

It's a strange courage
you give me, ancient star:

Shine alone in the sunrise
toward which you lend no part!

I

Shine alone, shine nakedly, shine like bronze,
that reflects neither my face nor any inner part
of my being, shine like fire, that mirrors nothing.

II

Lend no part to any humanity that suffuses
you in its own light.
Be not chimera of morning,
Half-man, half-star.
Be not an intelligence,
Like a widow's bird
Or an old horse.

nuances—*slight variations*
suffuses—*spreads over or through in the manner of light or liquid*
chimera—*a mythical beast*
intelligence—*the ability to learn or understand, but here meaning feeling*

PLOUGHING ON SUNDAY

Although Sunday is the Sabbath, the traditional day of rest, this poem celebrates the work of preparing the land for spring planting. Since Uncle Remus is told to toot his horn, could it be the work of telling stories or writing poems? The plough-man is excited and enthusiastic. Is it because he knows that people need poetry as much as they do food?

The white cock's tail
Tosses in the wind.
The turkey-cock's tail
Glitters in the sun.

Water in the fields.
The wind pours down.
The feathers flare
And bluster in the wind.

Remus, blow your horn!
I'm ploughing on Sunday,
Ploughing North America.
Blow your horn!

Tum-ti-tum,
Ti-tum-tum-tum!
The turkey-cock's tail
Spreads to the sun.

The white cock's tail
Streams to the moon.
Water in the fields.
The wind pours down.

Remus—*Uncle Remus, a character created by author Joel Chandler Harris, who tells folk tales about Brer Rabbit, Brer Fox, etc.*

HIBISCUS ON THE SLEEPING SHORES

*Have you ever spent a day at the beach and become so drowsy with
the heat of the sun that you were not even aware of the noise of the
ocean? Stevens captures this feeling by comparing the mind to a
moth that leaves the beach and wanders from flower to flower one
sleepy afternoon.*

I say now, Fernando, that on that day
The mind roamed as a moth roams,
Among the blooms beyond the open sand;

And that whatever noise the motion of the waves
Made on the sea-weeds and the covered stones
Disturbed not even the most idle ear.

Then it was that that monstered moth
Which had lain folded against the blue
And the colored purple of the lazy sea,

And which had drowsed along the bony shores,
Shut to the blather that the water made,
Rose up besprent and sought the flaming red

Dabbled with yellow pollen—red as red
As the flag above the old café—
And roamed there all the stupid afternoon.

Hibiscus—*a shrub or small tree with large, often red, flowers*
blather—*noisy nonsense*
besprent—*sprinkled over, as with water*
stupid—*dazed, stunned, or stupefied*

THE SNOW MAN

Imagine being a snowman, with eyes and mouth of coal, no ears, a carrot for a nose, and branches for arms and hands. What would happen to the world? Would it seem pleasant to you, or unpleasant? Would it even still exist, if you could not hear it, see it, smell it, taste it, or touch it? The word "snow man" sounds like "no man." Brrrrrrrrrrr!

One must have a mind of winter
To regard the frost and the boughs
Of the pine-trees crusted with snow;

And have been cold a long time
To behold the junipers shagged with ice,
The spruces rough in the distant glitter

Of the January sun; and not to think
Of any misery in the sound of the wind,
In the sound of a few leaves,

Which is the sound of the land
Full of the same wind
That is blowing in the same bare place

For the listener, who listens in the snow,
And, nothing himself, beholds
Nothing that is not there and the nothing that is.

DOMINATION OF BLACK

Nighttime can be scary. Sitting by a crackling fire, watching flickering shadows on the wall, listening to the wind outside blow the leaves about—you may well be frightened. Hearing the forlorn cry of peacocks (which sounds like "help! . . . help! . . . help!") would only add to your feeling of anxiety. Stevens fills this poem with dark images and eerie sounds to scare us. When someone asked him what the poem meant, he simply replied: "Its sole purpose is to fill the mind with the images & sounds that it contains . . . and you are supposed to feel as you would feel if you actually got all this." Do you feel afraid after reading this poem?

At night, by the fire,
The colors of the bushes
And of the fallen leaves,
Repeating themselves,
Turned in the room,
Like the leaves themselves
Turning in the wind.
Yes: but the color of the heavy hemlocks
Came striding.
And I remembered the cry of the peacocks.

The colors of their tails
Were like the leaves themselves
Turning in the wind,
In the twilight wind.
They swept over the room,
Just as they flew from the boughs of the hemlocks
Down to the ground.
I heard them cry—the peacocks.
Was it a cry against the twilight
Or against the leaves themselves
Turning in the wind,
Turning as the flames
Turned in the fire,
Turning as the tails of the peacocks
Turned in the loud fire,
Loud as the hemlocks
Full of the cry of the peacocks?
Or was it a cry against the hemlocks?

Out of the window,
I saw how the planets gathered
Like the leaves themselves
Turning in the wind.
I saw how the night came,
Came striding like the color of the heavy hemlocks.
I felt afraid.
And I remembered the cry of the peacocks.

hemlocks—*evergreen trees with short, flat needles*
striding—*taking long steps*

TEA AT THE PALAZ OF HOON

Stevens once admitted, "Poets are never lonely even when they pretend to be." Watching a sunset, the speaker felt as large and magnificent as the sun itself. But he knew that the beauty and wonder he experienced really came from within his own imagination. This made him feel less lonely, more truly himself, and more mysterious.

Not less because in purple I descended
The western day through what you called
The loneliest air, not less was I myself.

What was the ointment sprinkled on my beard?
What were the hymns that buzzed beside my ears?
What was the sea whose tide swept through me there?

Out of my mind the golden ointment rained,
And my ears made the blowing hymns they heard.
I was myself the compass of that sea:

I was the world in which I walked, and what I saw
Or heard or felt came not but from myself;
And there I found myself more truly and more strange.

Palaz—*palace*
ointment—*a soothing or healing cream*
compass—*extent, circumference*

ANECDOTE OF MEN BY THE THOUSAND

We can often tell where a person is from by the way he or she talks or dresses. Someone in a ten-gallon hat, blue jeans, and boots is most likely a Western cowboy, while someone who speaks with a soft, slow drawl is probably from the South. People are influenced by where they come from. This poem says that, but something more, too: the way people talk or dress expresses an important quality about their home.

The soul, he said, is composed
Of the external world.

There are men of the East, he said,
Who are the East.
There are men of a province
Who are that province.
There are men of a valley
Who are that valley.

There are men whose words
Are as natural sounds
Of their places
As the cackle of toucans
In the place of toucans.

The mandoline is the instrument
Of a place.

Are there mandolines of western mountains?
Are there mandolines of northern moonlight?

The dress of a woman of Lhassa,
In its place,
Is an invisible element of that place
Made visible.

toucans—*tropical birds with huge, brilliantly colored beaks*
mandoline—*a small, guitar-like stringed instrument; usually spelled mandolin*
Lhassa—*the capital of Tibet, now spelled Lhasa*

SIX SIGNIFICANT LANDSCAPES

Stevens had a strong interest in East Asia. He took great delight in Japanese prints and Chinese scrolls and kept a statue of Buddha in his room. He especially enjoyed exhibitions of Chinese landscape painting. This poem takes us on an imaginary tour of such an exhibit, where we view six landscapes painted in words, mostly in the Chinese style. These landscapes suggest unity among all things. They invite us to see the universe from a different, Eastern, viewpoint.

I

An old man sits
In the shadow of a pine tree
In China.
He sees larkspur,
Blue and white,
At the edge of the shadow,
Move in the wind.
His beard moves in the wind.
The pine tree moves in the wind.
Thus water flows
Over weeds.

II

The night is of the color
Of a woman's arm:
Night, the female,
Obscure,
Fragrant and supple,
Conceals herself.
A pool shines,
Like a bracelet
Shaken in a dance.

larkspur—*a flower with many blossoms on its stem*

III

I measure myself
Against a tall tree.
I find that I am much taller,
For I reach right up to the sun,
With my eye;
And I reach to the shore of the sea
With my ear.
Nevertheless, I dislike
The way the ants crawl
In and out of my shadow.

IV

When my dream was near the moon,
The white folds of its gown
Filled with yellow light.
The soles of its feet
Grew red.
Its hair filled
With certain blue crystallizations
From stars,
Not far off.

crystallizations—*coated with crystals; glass-like*

V

Not all the knives of the lamp-posts,
Nor the chisels of the long streets,
Nor the mallets of the domes
And high towers,
Can carve
What one star can carve,
Shining through the grape-leaves.

VI

Rationalists, wearing square hats,
Think, in square rooms,
Looking at the floor,
Looking at the ceiling.
They confine themselves
To right-angled triangles.
If they tried rhomboids,
Cones, waving lines, ellipses—
As, for example, the ellipse of the half-moon—
Rationalists would wear sombreros.

mallets—*light hammers with small, rounded or spherical heads*
Rationalists—*people who rely exclusively on reason*
rhomboids—*similar to tilting rectangles, but having no right*
   angles and lines of uneven length
ellipses—*ovals, curved like somewhat flattened circles*

GUBBINAL

The speaker fools the fool in this poem! He pretends to agree with a person who thinks the world is dreary. But he really thinks the opposite. By describing the sun in fresh and vivid images, the speaker mocks the person who cannot see the magical variety of life. That person is really the sad one!

That strange flower, the sun,
Is just what you say.
Have it your way.

The world is ugly,
And the people are sad.

That tuft of jungle feathers,
That animal eye,
Is just what you say.

That savage of fire,
That seed,
Have it your way.

The world is ugly,
And the people are sad.

Gubbinal—*slang for fool; also, anything of little value*

39

THE EMPEROR OF ICE-CREAM

Poets often call attention to the preciousness of life by contrasting it with death. The two stanzas here represent two rooms, one with pleasurable activity and the other with death. In the kitchen, a strong man is asked to make ice cream by hand, the old-fashioned way. In the bedroom lies a woman who has died. Have the girls and boys come to show respect for the woman or to enjoy ice cream, or both? The energetic tone and exciting sounds express a positive attitude toward life—all those k sounds in "whip / In kitchen cups concupiscent curds" seemingly whip words into ice cream. Stevens selected this poem as one of his favorites because, he said, it was "an instance of letting myself go."

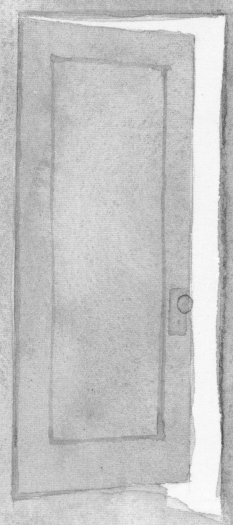

Call the roller of big cigars,
The muscular one, and bid him whip
In kitchen cups concupiscent curds.
Let the wenches dawdle in such dress
As they are used to wear, and let the boys
Bring flowers in last month's newspapers.
Let be be finale of seem.
The only emperor is the emperor of ice-cream.

Take from the dresser of deal,
Lacking the three glass knobs, that sheet
On which she embroidered fantails once
And spread it so as to cover her face.
If her horny feet protrude, they come
To show how cold she is, and dumb.
Let the lamp affix its beam.
The only emperor is the emperor of ice-cream.

concupiscent—*strongly desirable, pronounced kän-kyoo'-pa-sent*
curds—*thickened milk; in this case, ice cream*
wenches—*young poor girls, such as servants*
Let be be finale of seem—*let what is be the end of something not real or not true*
deal—*cheap wooden boards*
fantails—*a pattern resembling the tail feathers of a fantail pigeon*
horny—*calloused or hardened spots on one's feet*

A Rabbit as King of the Ghosts

Sometimes the world can seem threatening to us during the day, but at night, alone in our room, we feel secure and confident. Stevens uses the images of an aggressive cat and a gentle rabbit to express that mood. At night, when the threatening cat is gone, the rabbit feels safe and at peace. At home in his world, he feels like a king, while the cat seems insignificant by comparison.

The difficulty to think at the end of day,
When the shapeless shadow covers the sun
And nothing is left except light on your fur—

There was the cat slopping its milk all day,
Fat cat, red tongue, green mind, white milk
And August the most peaceful month.

To be, in the grass, in the peacefullest time,
Without that monument of cat,
The cat forgotten in the moon;

And to feel that the light is a rabbit-light,
In which everything is meant for you
And nothing need be explained;

Then there is nothing to think of. It comes
        of itself;
And east rushes west and west rushes down,
No matter. The grass is full

And full of yourself. The trees around are
        for you,
The whole of the wideness of night
        is for you,
A self that touches all edges,

You become a self that fills the four corners of night.
The red cat hides away in the fur-light
And there you are humped high, humped up,

You are humped higher and higher, black as stone—
You sit with your head like a carving in space
And the little green cat is a bug in the grass.

TATTOO

Have you ever noticed something as commonplace as light? Stevens uses an unusual comparison to freshen our awareness of it. Much like a spider casting a web, light connects us to the physical world. But if the light, in the form of the spider's web, touches us, we are connected to it, too!

The light is like a spider.
It crawls over the water.
It crawls over the edges of the snow.
It crawls under your eyelids
And spreads its webs there—
Its two webs.

The webs of your eyes
Are fastened
To the flesh and bones of you
As to rafters or grass.

There are filaments of your eyes
On the surface of the water
And in the edges of the snow.

rafters—*a framework of boards used to support a roof*
filaments—*thin wires or threadlike material capable of carrying light or an electric current*

44

THE DEATH OF A SOLDIER

During World War I, Stevens read a book of letters written by a French
soldier to his mother. The thoughts of the young man inspired
Stevens to write a series of poems about war. In one
letter, the soldier had written, "La mort du soldat est
près des choses naturelles." ("The death of a solider
is almost a natural thing.") Stevens used the
season of autumn, when we expect leaves to
fall, to communicate this feeling.

Life contracts and death is expected,
As in a season of autumn.
The soldier falls.

He does not become a three-days personage,
Imposing his separation,
Calling for pomp.

Death is absolute and without memorial,
As in a season of autumn,
When the wind stops,

When the wind stops and,
    over the heavens,
The clouds go,
    nevertheless,
In their direction.

personage—*an important person*
pomp—*a showy ceremony*

45

THE HOUSE WAS QUIET AND THE WORLD WAS CALM

Have you ever been so wrapped up in a book that the actual world disappeared? Stevens captures that mood through the music of this poem. The long, rhythmic lines arranged in couplets and the frequent repetition create a songlike quality that draws us into the poem. Like the speaker, we settle into a moment of tranquility, a sense of perfect fulfillment.

The house was quiet and the world was calm.
The reader became the book; and summer night

Was like the conscious being of the book.
The house was quiet and the world was calm.

The words were spoken as if there was no book,
Except that the reader leaned above the page,

Wanted to lean, wanted much most to be
The scholar to whom his book is true, to whom

The summer night is like a perfection of thought.
The house was quiet because it had to be.

The quiet was part of the meaning, part of the mind:
The access of perfection to the page.

And the world was calm. The truth in a calm world,
In which there is no other meaning, itself

Is calm, itself is summer and night, itself
Is the reader leaning late and reading there.

conscious being—*alive with self-awareness of thought or observation; personally felt*
access—*entry*

INDEX